ABOUT THIS BOOK

MY WAR WITH MRS. GALLOWAY
By Doris Orgel
Illustrated by Carol Newsom

It's six-fifteen, the time Rebecca waits for all day long!
That's when her favorite M.D. (Mom Doctor) gets
home, and they can share their special time. It's also
when Mrs. Galloway leaves. Rebecca has seen lots of
babysitters come and go, but Mrs. Galloway is the
worst. She gets mad at everything! She didn't think it
was at all funny when Rebecca and her friend Michael
covered the entire bathroom with vanishing cream.
The mess should have just disappeared anyway. And
she didn't like Becca's portrait of "Mrs. Gallopaway"
riding on her crazy horse. But now she is always mean
to Becca's cat, Whiskers—and Whiskers is having
kittens! That means war!

MY WAR WITH MRS. GALLOWAY

BY DORIS ORGEL

Mrs. Gallopaway

Illustrated by Carol Newsom

Puffin Books

Remembering Erna Adelberg

PUFFIN BOOKS

Viking Penguin Inc., 40 West 23rd Street, New York, New York 10010, U.S.A.
Penguin Books Ltd, Harmondsworth, Middlesex, England
Penguin Books Australia Ltd, Ringwood, Victoria, Australia
Penguin Books Canada Limited, 2801 John Street, Markham, Ontario, Canada L3R 1B4
Penguin Books (N.Z.) Ltd, 182–190 Wairau Road, Auckland 10, New Zealand

First published by Viking Penguin Inc. 1985
Published in Puffin Books 1986
Reprinted 1987
Text copyright © Doris Orgel, 1985
Illustrations copyright © Carol Newsom, 1985
All rights reserved
Printed in U.S.A. by R. R. Donnelley & Sons Company, Harrisonburg, Virginia
Set in Sabon Roman

Library of Congress Cataloging in Publication Data
Orgel, Doris.   My war with Mrs. Galloway.
Summary: Eight-year-old Rebecca, whose divorced mother
is a doctor, has an ongoing war with her babysitter,
Mrs. Galloway, until one day the two reach an unexpected truce.
[1. Babysitters—Fiction.   2. Single-parent family—
Fiction]   I. Newsom, Carol, ill.   II. Title.
PZ7.O632My   1986   [Fic]   86-4876   ISBN 0-14-032171-3

Contents

My War with Mrs. Galloway

Six-Fifteen

Six-fifteen—the time I wait for, all day long!

When it gets to be around six-twelve or six-thirteen, I put my ear against the wall in our foyer. That way I can hear the elevator when it starts to hum. There, it's starting to!

I race out to the landing. The numbers over the elevator door light up—2, 3, 4. Now it reaches 5—that's our floor! The door slides open. Out she comes, Naomi Suslow, M.D., stethoscope sticking up from her pocket, pretty hair bouncing around her face.

She holds her arms out. I fly into them. She lifts me up. My nose smells hospital and lilacs. I love that smell. It's Mom-perfume. "Hey, Mom Doc, you're home!"

When I was little I used to think "M.D." stood for "Mom Doctor." Then I found out that all doctors have those letters after their names, whether they're anyone's moms, dads, or not.

"Hey, Becca"—that's her private name for me—"what kind of day did you have?"

"It was okay. *Now* it's getting good."

We go inside our apartment. Our private time begins. We sit together in the blue velvet armchair with white daisies on it, in the foyer. Just Mom and me, us two. Or just us three, if Whiskers jumps up. We like it when she does that. She's welcome on our laps.

Mrs. Galloway is supposed to leave now. But she takes forever putting on her coat, finding her umbrella, tying on her scarf. She interrupts our private time by asking, "Is it windy out? Does it look like rain?"

Mom answers her politely. "Not too windy. Yes, it looks as if it might rain."

"Don't forget," Mrs. Galloway goes on, "there's an open can of Tunafeast in the refrigerator"—which Whiskers will never eat! Whiskers despises Tunafeast. When will Mrs. Galloway get that through her head?

Finally she's ready. She goes out the door—only to come right in again. She's forgotten her galoshes. She looks in the closet. There's only one galosh in there.

Mom gets out of our chair to help hunt for the other.

Right at this moment I hate Mrs. Galloway, and I feel like we're fighting a war.

She shoots me a look that says, You know darn well where that other galosh is!

Yes, now I remember. I go and get it. I hand it to her. "Here."

She bends down, puts it on. It makes a little *squish* sound (because it was in the bathtub). She doesn't hear it, I guess. And now she really does leave. Phew! Good night, at last!

If she had heard the galosh go *squish*, she'd

have told Mom, See what that kid of yours and that pal of hers, Michael, did? They took my galosh without asking. They got it wet, used it for goodness knows what! (We used it for a flotation device during splashdown. We were playing Space Shuttle.)

And Mom would have gotten mad at me. Maybe she wouldn't have sat back down in the velvet armchair. And I'd have had to wait— all tonight, all tomorrow morning, all tomorrow afternoon—for six-fifteen to come around again.

FAWWWGH!

Mom says we found Mrs. Galloway "by great good luck."

"Great good luck," my eye! It's been war since the day she came.

The first day I showed her around the apartment, right away she did something mean to Whiskers.

Whiskers is our cat. We found her on the roof. Mom keeps flowerpots up there. One time in the summer, when we were planting

8

petunias, who should come out from behind
the brick smokestack but a beautiful, skinny,
shiny black cat with white paws and hind legs
white up to her knees, almost as if she had
knee socks on, and with a white patch around
her mouth and chin. It was Whiskers. We put
up a Cat Found sign in the basement laundry
room, but nobody claimed her. So we kept
her.

Whiskers likes to lie on top of the refrigerator. I think the soft buzzing noise the refrigerator motor makes sounds like company
to her, like another cat purring right along.

"That's no place for a cat," said Mrs. Galloway, the first day, and she stuck out her arm.
She's very tall, so she could reach up there
easily. And she swept Whiskers down.

It's pretty far to fall. Cats are supposed to
always land on their feet. But Whiskers looked
like she might not, while she was in the air. I
couldn't breathe, I was so scared for her.

She did land on her feet. She licked herself
in a few places.

Mrs. Galloway bent down to her.

Whiskers bared her teeth: *FAWWWGH!* I agreed. I knew just what she meant.

Mrs. G. said, "Don't you *fawwwgh* at me!"

Whiskers shot away, like an arrow, straight into my room. She can still run fast, even with her heavy belly. And she hid in the drawer where my sweaters are. I usually keep it a little bit open. She likes to nuzzle in there when I'm not home and she's lonely, or when her feelings are hurt.

Mrs. Galloway said, "Rebecca, from now on, keep that drawer shut."

"Why?"

"Because I'll be washing those sweaters of yours. And you don't want them full of cat hairs, do you?"

"Yes."

She shook her head at me. She reached into the drawer and dumped Whiskers out.

I picked Whiskers up and held her. "You hate cats," I said.

Mrs. Galloway has straggly eyebrows. One of them went up. She looked like she was laughing to herself. "I don't hate cats," she

said. "I just don't think they belong on tops of refrigerators or in sweater drawers."

Well, I disagreed, and as soon as Mrs. Galloway went out of my room, I let Whiskers right back in my drawer. I covered her up with my best, softest sweater. She purred. She belonged in there, all right. She belonged wherever she wanted to be, in this whole apartment.

And Mrs. Galloway didn't!

Before
Mrs. Galloway

I never had a war with any other sitter.

Mrs. Galloway's been here a month. Before, my sitter was Emily Rothstein. She was really more of a sprawler—on her stomach, on the couch, or on the floor, with her sneakers up in the air. With the TV or radio on, full blast. That's how she studied, studied, studied—economics, statistics, and other hard subjects ending in "ics." She studied all the time.

One time my friend Michael and I were lapping up cream from two saucers on the kitchen floor to see who could lap the fastest. Whiskers sat up on the counter eating a bologna sandwich. Just the bologna—she left the bread on the plate. Well, Emily Rothstein came into the kitchen. And she didn't even notice. She just took a Tab out of the refrigerator and went back to studying "ics."

Another time, I sailed all my old boats in the bathtub. I made a huge storm, with high waves and a downpour (from the shower), to see which boats would capsize and which would sail on. Well, Mr. Riordan, the super, came up. He said water was dripping through the Nagels' ceiling. They live right under us. And when Mom got home, Mrs. Nagel came up and complained.

So then Mom had a talk with me, saying that I shouldn't do such things. And she had a talk with Emily. She said she understood that Emily needed to study. She just thought that Emily should also try to watch me more. Emily said she would.

Before Emily Rothstein, let me see: I had Mrs. Finkel. Mrs. Finkel taught me Gin Rummy. She really loved that game. She could play a hundred hands of it and still want to play more.

Before her, I had Mrs. Aiello. "I-yell-oh" is how you said her name. So, at first, I felt a little scared of her. But she never even raised her voice. If anything, she talked too baby-ingly, and called me things like Duck and Cutie-Pie. She was my first during-the-day sitter.

Before Mrs. Aiello, I didn't need daytime sitters. Because Dad still lived with us, and stayed with me, and took me with him wher-ever he went.

My father is a painter. Painting pictures is his real job. But he also painted apartments and houses, inside and out. He did that to earn money while Mom went to medical school. And I went along, even when I was still really little. I can kind of remember, way way back, lying on my baby blanket, on some grass, look-ing up at his white overall legs with blue sky between them. He stood up on a ladder.

His head was near the clouds.

When I got bigger, he showed me how to dip the roller in paint. (Paint is another smell I like a real lot.) And I didn't just pretend-help, I really painted right along with him, the bottoms of walls and the windowsills.

At home he had a big, tall easel in the living room. One time we were horsing around and I knocked it over. Paint got on the floor. And the picture he was working on—it was of the Brooklyn Bridge—got messed up. So he painted over the messy parts and made it even better. We still have that picture. It's hanging in my room.

When I was in kindergarten, he moved to Portland, Oregon. Mom and I live in Brooklyn, New York. He and Mom got divorced. Brooklyn, New York, and Portland, Oregon, are the whole width of America apart.

But on my sixth and seventh birthdays— surprise! Dad came to visit. It was great.

He can't make it back here often. But we write each other letters and we talk on the phone. He's saving up for my air fare. Mom's saving up, too. And someday I'll fly out there and visit him.

Anyway, here's why Emily Rothstein is not my sitter anymore. One afternoon, Mom called up from the hospital where she works. She wanted to speak to me. And Emily didn't know where I was. I'd told her where we were going. But I guess she wasn't listening.

Michael and I were up on the roof. It's safe, Mom lets me. We'd brought some bread up there to feed the pigeons. Michael also brought a Baggie full of water to drop down on his enemy, Tom Spindell, in case Tom walked by below. Tom didn't. So we built a drinking fountain for pigeons and poured the water in there.

When Emily couldn't find me, Mom got worried—she thought I was lost. She rushed home from the hospital, and found me right away, because I saw her park the car, and I waved and yelled, "Mom, Mom, look up here!"

She was glad to see me but sorry she'd rushed home. Because the sick people at the hospital really needed her. Rushing home should be saved for real emergencies. She explained this to Emily Rothstein. Then she fired her.

Then, for a week, I didn't have any sitter. And Mom couldn't take time off from the hospital. And Grandma Sonia couldn't leave her job to come take care of me, either. So, for that whole week, after school I went home with Michael. He lives down the hall in 5G, and I've known him since we were babies.

It was nice of Michael's mom to let me come. The first two afternoons, it worked out okay. But on Wednesday Tom Spindell came over, too. He and Michael had made up. And they only played with each other, and they left me out. I pretended I didn't care.

Thursday, Michael and I got into a fight. Both those afternoons I wished I could go home.

Then Mom found Mrs. Galloway.

Mom was really happy. Mrs. Galloway was not only going to be my sitter but would also do things around the apartment, like clean and buy food. So Mom would have less of those things to do when she got home, and more time just to be with me.

Mom asked me to be on my best behavior so that Mrs. Galloway would like the job and would want to stay.

I tried, I really did. But then she made Whiskers get down from on top of the refrigerator, and our war began.

Truce

Michael is my ally in the war with Mrs. Galloway. One time, when she was really mad at us, he tried to make her disappear. I kind of knew it wouldn't work. "If you were *my* kids, I'd wallop you, good!" she yelled at us as loud as thunder. And she made Michael go home.

We'd been playing Magician. We'd made a pretty big mess. I didn't tell Mom. I figured she'd hear about it soon enough from Mrs. Galloway. The only thing is, Mrs. G. hasn't told her yet. I wonder when she will. . . .

The only bad thing about Michael is, he acts pretty bossy sometimes. For instance, about his steering wheel.

It's a real subway steering wheel, made of iron, big and heavy. It used to be in an old subway train, in the front car, inside the little booth where the motorman sits and makes the train go. Michael's father got it for him. Michael has a great big walk-in closet. It's almost like another room inside his room. His father attached the steering wheel to the closet wall. When the light is out in there, it's really like the subway. Michael sits at the wheel on a tall stool, and wears his motorman cap, and *he's* the motorman. Every time we play Subway. All I ever get to be is the subway riders.

Last time, I said, "No fair, Michael. I should have a turn. I'll be the motorwoman."

" 'Motorwoman,' ha, ha, ha! There is no such thing!"

I said, "Yes, there is."

"There is not. Want to bet? Mom, Mom, come in here!"

Michael's mom came in. With their baby, Amanda, riding on her hip. Michael said, "Mom, is there such a thing as a motor-woman, ha, ha, ha?"

She said, "Not funny, Michael. Sure there is—why not? Motorman, motorwoman—what's the difference? Now, you give Becky a turn at the wheel. Or else."

"Or else what?"

"I'll disattach it."

Michael looked as though he doubted she would do that.

She said, "I'll go get the screwdriver, right now. I'll have it out of here faster than you can say 'motorperson.' "

"No, Mom!"

He let me have a turn.

I steered the subway train over the part where it goes above ground, over the bridge from Brooklyn to Manhattan. I held the wheel straight and firm. I loved the idea that I was making the whole train stay on its tracks.

But then Michael ruined it. He turned the light off in the closet. He shouted, "This train is going out of service! All subway riders off this train!"

"Michael, they can't! The train's over the East River!"

"Says who? *I* say, everybody off the train." And he wouldn't turn the light back on.

I got disgusted with the whole thing. I said, "You're just jealous. You can't stand it when you're not the motorman." And I went home.

"Had a fight with Michael?" asked Mrs. Galloway.

He was still my ally, so I didn't say. I just asked her, "Do you think there could be such a thing as a motorperson?"

She said, "You mean, a woman subway driver?" For once, she acted kind of understanding. And for just a short while, our war stopped and we had a truce. She told me that when she was little—which it's hard to imagine she ever was—her mother worked in a grocery store. She supposed that made her mother a grocery-store person, though nobody ever called her that. "But there could be such a thing. And there could be a motorperson, sure."

Just then, Whiskers jumped up on the table.

"Get down, you sassy thing!" She whisked her off. That was the end of our truce.

I said, "You shouldn't do that to her."

"Why not, may I ask?"

"Because you could hurt her, or her kittens inside."

She gave me a mean laugh. "Not likely. Don't you worry yourself about 'her kittens inside.' " She imitated my voice saying that. "Here, do something useful for a change, help me fold this sheet."

But I didn't. Our war was on again.

How Many Kittens?

Whiskers was up on our laps. I put my hand under her belly. I could feel the kittens moving around. But I couldn't tell where one left off and another began.

I asked Mom, "How many kittens do you think she has in there?"

Mom felt. She said, "Well, it's her first litter and she's pretty small. Not too many, I would guess."

"Mom, how many can we—?"

"Becca"—Mom made a pretend-tired face—
"please don't ask me that question *again.*"

I couldn't help it. "How many can we keep?"

She let out a sigh. "I wish I had a kiss for
every time you've asked me that."

I gave her a bunch of kisses.

"Mm, good. But the answer's still the same:
one. One kitten, plus Whiskers, plus us, is
plenty."

"But what if she has three—or four? Please,
Mom, please, can't we keep more of
them?"

"We'll keep them all till they're weaned."

I know, I know, weaned means when they're
ready to drink milk from a saucer instead of
sucking it from Whiskers's nipples. Cat mothers nurse kittens the same way human mothers
nurse babies. Except cat mothers have eight
nipples, and humans only two. I said, "Mom,
what will we do with the ones we don't
keep?"

"We'll give them to people. Don't worry."

I did, though. I thought, Suppose she has
four kittens and we only find two people be-

sides us who'll want one? What'll happen to the one left over?

I called up Grandma Sonia. She said she would love a kitten. The only trouble was, Elmo, her Labrador retriever, might not like it, might be rough with it. So she thought, Better not.

Then I got this other idea: maybe Dad could take one. He lives in a house now, not just an apartment. And he has a back yard, and a garden out in front. Also, he likes animals.

Mom said the air fare for an animal is almost as much as for a person. And flying out there all alone, cooped up in a crate, would be hard for a very young kitten. She didn't think I should call him. I'd called him just the night before. And we have to watch our phone bill.

I said, "Please, Mom! I really need to talk to him."

Whenever I say that, in just that voice, she ends up letting me.

She was fixing dinner. There's a phone right in the kitchen. But she knows it's hard for me to talk to Dad with anybody else around, even if it's her. "Use the phone in my room," she said.

First you punch the number 1. Then the area code: 503. Then the rest of the number. I know it by heart: 555-1717. I did it in a hurry. I must have goofed it up somehow. Because a little squeaky voice came on: "Hello?"

I asked, "Who's this?"

"Hope!"

Nobody by that name lived at Dad's house. "Hope who?"

"Hope you hang up and don't call again!" squeaked the voice and giggled like crazy. Isn't that dumb?

I know I should have called the credit office and said I'd reached the wrong number so we wouldn't be charged for the call. But I was too embarrassed.

I tried again. I was careful with the numbers. This time, Dad came on. We had a good talk. But Mom was right, he said, an airplane ticket for a kitten would cost too much, and wouldn't I rather he saved the money for *my* ticket to Portland?

I said, "Yes. When, Dad? How about for my eighth birthday?"

He said, "Maybe. We'll see." He sounded like he thought eight years old isn't old enough to fly all that distance on my own.

"You sound kind of sad, Dad."

"Well, I miss you, Becky-Boo"—that's his special name for me.

I said, "Ditto, ditto, Dad-O!"

Flying to Saskatchewan

I was over at Michael's. His mom was working in the bedroom, writing a book. Amanda, the baby, was sleeping.

Michael and I'd already played Donkey Kong (he has a small hand game of it). We'd played Subway and Explorers, and Michael couldn't think of what to play next. I said, "How about Divorce?"

"How do you play that?"

"I'll be the woman, you be the husband—"

"No! It sounds like House! I'm not playing any stupid baby game like that."

"It's not like House. It's just the opposite."

"Okay, what do I do?"

"You're leaving. Start packing up your things."

He went and got a suitcase. He put in rolled-up pairs of socks from his bureau drawer. "Shouldn't we fight, first?"

"We don't have to."

But he wanted to. So we did, throwing the rolled-up socks at each other. That part was fun.

"Now what do we do?" he asked.

"Finish packing. Here." I handed him his motorman cap. He put it in the suitcase. Also, undershirts, some cars, and his New York Mets sweatshirt.

"Ready? Come on, I'll drive you to the airport. You have to catch a plane."

"Where to?" he asked me. "Portland, Oregon?"

"No, dummy, Portland isn't the only place people fly to."

"Hey, you don't have to get so mad."

Yes, I had to. What did he think? That my father is the only person who ever flew away anywhere? And that I only wanted to play this whole game on account of him and Mom? Plenty of people get divorced, all the time, didn't he realize that? I said, "There are millions of places. Just think of one you want to live in."

"Okay, I will, take it easy. *I* know—Saskatchewan."

"Where's that?"

"Up in Canada."

"Okay." I drove him to the airport. He caught the plane.

"Now can we play something else?" he wanted to know.

"Not yet. You like it there. The air is better, there's more room, you feel more like yourself there. You find a place to live. Everything's terrific. Except, you miss our child."

Michael still has a teddy bear, I happen to know. Because when I came to see him after he had his tonsils out, he had the teddy right in bed with him. I looked under his pillow. There it was, with a red ribbon around its neck.

"Hey!" Michael turned almost as red as the teddy's ribbon. He grabbed it away from me, stuck the pillow over it.

I said, "Relax, I won't tell anybody you still have it. Just let the teddy fly out to Saskatchewan to visit you, okay?"

"No! This game is worse than House!"

Just then Amanda woke up—we could hear her crying. Their mom called, "Michael, come in here, please. Keep Amanda company for a couple of minutes while I finish this page."

I know this was babyish of me: while Michael was out of the room, I packed a little suitcase for the teddy and I drove him to the airport. I got him settled on the plane. I asked the lady sitting in the next seat to keep an eye on him. And the teddy flew to Saskatchewan.

When I heard Michael coming back, I quickly put the teddy back under the pillow. *Brrrm*— I raced two cars across the floor, pretending I'd been doing that the whole time. I said,

"Listen, Michael, I've been meaning to ask you something."

"What? Ask me."

"When Whiskers has her kittens, and after they're weaned, would you like to have one?"

"Sure! I'd love one. How about two, if she has a whole lot of them?"

"Yes, that would be great. Of course you have to ask your mother."

I didn't mean right then. But he rushed right in to her. I went along.

She was in the middle of putting a Pamper on Amanda, who was lying on the bureau top, crying and kicking her legs as hard as she could.

"Mom," Michael asked, "when Becky's cat has kittens, can we take one? Or how about two?"

"A kitten? *Two* kittens?" She had to shout really loud because Amanda was going like a fire engine. "Are you out of your mind? Can't you see I have my hands full enough? The answer's no. *Absoposolutely Not!*"

Mrs. Gallopaway

When I got home, Mrs. Galloway said, "You look as though you have the whole world's troubles on your shoulders." And she wanted to know what I was worrying about.

"What'll happen to" —I was going to say "the kittens," but I figured she wouldn't care. "Oh, nothing. What time is it, anyway?"

"Five after four."

Two more hours and ten more minutes— one hundred thirty trips the minute hand had to take around the clockface before Mom got home. "Come on," I called to Whiskers and started to go to my room.

I guess Mrs. G. wanted another little truce. She put her hand on my head, kind of gently. "Cheer up," she said in a nice voice, and I started to think, She can be nice when she tries.

But, next thing, she wrecked it—by calling me Becca! Who did she think she was—Mom?

I really hated her for that. I ran into my room. I flew onto my bed. I hammered on my white bedspread with my fists and with my shoes on. Who cared if it got dirty?

I thought, Too bad the vanishing cream hadn't worked on Mrs. Galloway that day. . . . I wished she'd vanish right off the face of the earth. Why couldn't there be a way to make that happen? *Whomp, clomp* went my heels on the bedspread.

I thought of when Dad got into terrible moods. He's got a temper like mine. And how, in the middle of being mad, he'd grab a sketch-pad and pencil. One time he couldn't find a pad, so he took a brown grocery bag from the supermarket and made it smooth and painted on it, big splotches of paint, which turned out wild, but good.

I went to my desk. I got out my crayons and paper. I drew this picture:

Her teeth are not really that yellow. But white didn't show up on the paper. Her nose is not that much like a potato. Her chin's not that long, but so what? She doesn't have a horse, either. But I put her on one. I let her hair fly all over the place, to show that the wind is blowing. And the horse has all four legs off the ground to show he's going fast.

Underneath I printed in big purple letters: MRS. GALLOPAWAY

When I was done, she was standing over me. She'd tiptoed in, really quietly, while I was working on the picture.

"Hm," she said. Not "My, what an inter-
esting picture," which is what grown-ups say
when they don't understand what you drew.
She understood, all right. She didn't say "You
spelled my name wrong." She knows I'm a
good speller and that I spelled it just the way
I meant. "Hm." Just "Hm." And her straggly
eyebrows pulled together, making more wrin-
kles on her forehead than she has, anyway.
Usually she stands up as straight as a stick.
Now her shoulders slumped, and she walked
out of the room.

After a couple of minutes, I followed her
into the living room. I was going to say I'd
draw a better picture of her if she wanted me
to, or something like that.

But she sat with her back to me, looking at
the TV, which wasn't on, and didn't turn
around. So I went back in my room.

I guess, in our war, this was a battle I won
over her, and she ended up feeling bad. The
funny thing is, I didn't feel too great about it,
either. . . .

Nightmare Night

That night I had a nightmare. I fell out of the sky. I just kept falling and falling, through all-the-way darkness, no stars, no moon.

Mom came in. She turned the light on.

I told it to her.

She brought me a drink of water.

She tucked me in, like when I was little. "Go back to sleep now. Have a happier dream. Want your glasses on?" She handed them to me. And she gave me our old secret smile from

when I first got them (I was around five) and
I thought I needed them on at night or I wouldn't
see my dreams.

I said, "No, Mom."

"Are you sure?"

I said, "Sure." But I couldn't give her back
the smile.

She sat down on my bed. She said in her
song-soft night-voice, "Becca, tell me what's
wrong."

"Oh, Mom—!" And things spilled out, all
jumbled. About what if, when the kittens were
born, there was one too many that nobody
would want? About Mrs. Galloway, too. "You
think she's so good, Mom. Well, she isn't.
There's not one good thing about her. She's
awful—not just to me, but to Whiskers and
Michael. . . .

Out spilled the whole story of when we
played Magician. "One time, last week, Michael had his hat on—the pointy one from
Halloween, with silver moons and stars on it.
You know, his magician's hat. We were in the
bathroom. There was this jar of vanishing

cream—yours, Mom. He took it down. He said, 'What's this for?'

" 'It makes your skin feel smooth,' I said. I put some on his hand.

"He asked, 'Why is it called "vanishing"?'

" 'Because when you rub it, it vanishes into your skin.' I rubbed some in. 'See?'

"He said, 'No, I don't see anything.'

" 'That's because it vanished.'

"He said, 'Great!' He was the magician. I was the helper, as usual. He said, 'Let's see what else this stuff can make vanish.'

"I said, 'Don't be dumb. It can't make stuff vanish, only itself.'

"He said, 'Let's try, anyway, just for fun.'

"I didn't really want to, Mom. But then he put the hat on me and said, '*You* be the magician.' And he whispered in my ear, 'Maybe it can make *people* vanish—like, for instance, you know who.' And he said, '*Abracadabra.* Come on, Becky, say it with me.' So I said it, too. And we put vanishing cream on just a few things, Mom. . . . "

Mom asked, "What things?"

"Oh, just some combs. And on my hair-brush. On the tooth mug, on the mirror, on the toilet seat cover. Michael wanted to try some on Whiskers's whiskers, too. I said, 'No. Absoposolutely not.' That's a word his mother uses.

"Then Mrs. Galloway banged on the door and yelled, 'What are you two doing in there?' Mom, she's against being in the bathroom with another person! She's even against being in there with just a cat!

"She banged so hard, I let her in. 'Michael, don't!' I whispered. He had gobs of vanishing cream on his hands. I knew it wouldn't work. He jumped at her and splatted it on her dress.

"She wiped it off and yelled the thing she always yells: 'If you were my kids, I'd wallop you, good.' She made us wipe the vanishing cream off the combs, the brush, the tooth mug, the mirror, the toilet seat cover, the floor. She was so mad at us! She said that the stuff we wasted was expensive and we'd better start saving up our allowances so we can buy you

another jar, Mom. We're doing that. Mom, are you mad?"

Mom said, "It's too late in the night to get mad at you. But I don't think she acted that awful."

"Wait, I haven't told you everything. She pushed Whiskers down off the bathroom windowsill. She's always pushing her down from places. Couldn't that hurt the kittens?"

Mom said, "I doubt it. They're pretty well protected inside her. What else?"

"Mom, she called me Becca! Doesn't she realize that name is reserved and only you can call me it?"

Mom said, "You could explain that to her in a nice way. Or I will, if you want me to."

"Yes. No. Because then she'll know I told you—"

"That's true," said Mom. "Well, sleep on it." She kissed me goodnight on my nose, cheeks, and eyelids.

I snuggled under the covers. The dark on the inside of my eyelids turned velvet-soft, like when you're about to go to sleep. If you think of something right around then, it's the truth, and it's important. Well, I thought of this: there *was* one good thing about Mrs. Galloway—she hadn't told on me. Not about the vanishing cream. Or about the other things, like that there was water in her galosh, or about my picture of her galloping away. . . .

Trying to Be Nicer

The first thing you think of when you wake up in the morning can also be important, and the truth. Here's what I thought: not telling on people matters. It's really a very good thing.

I asked Mom, "Don't say anything to Mrs. Galloway, okay?"

"Okay." Mom was happy not to.

I decided I would try being nicer to Mrs. Galloway. Because she hadn't told on me. And because maybe that way she'd be a little nicer back.

Mom gave me a present that morning before she left for work—her stethoscope, to keep! I was thrilled. "But how will you listen to people's hearts now?"

She said she has another stethoscope at the hospital.

You can listen to animals' hearts with it, too. I tried it on Whiskers. But she wouldn't hold still. The way you do it is, you stick the round part on the person's—or animal's—chest, and you stick the two little ear things in your ears, and you hear the heart go *pa-boom*, *pa-boom*, pretty loud, right in your ears.

That afternoon when I got home from school I showed it to Mrs. G. and I asked her very nicely, "Would you like me to listen to your heart?"

"Well, okay." Then she got all suspicious. "But don't ask me to take off any clothes. I don't approve of that."

She is so old-fashioned! She had a sweater on, and under it a dress, and under it a slip,

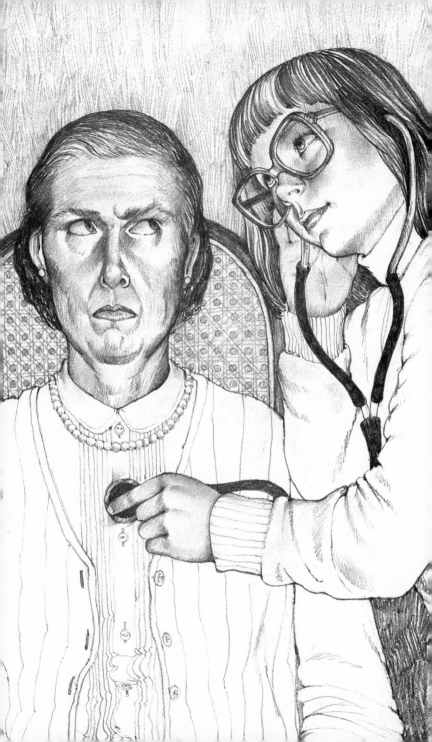

a brassiere, and probably an undershirt, too.

I tried to listen through all those clothes.

"Is it beating all right?" she asked.

"I guess so." But I wasn't sure. I couldn't really hear it.

I went to Michael's. I showed him how to use the stethoscope. We played Extra-Galactic Medical Research Project. The closet was our Space Lab Module. Different kinds of humanoids and animaloids from galaxies that haven't been discovered yet came to us for checkups.

The humanoids and animaloids were all different shapes and colors. Michael got a good idea. He took out his Craypas, and we made ourselves look a little more like our patients, so they would feel more at home with us. We colored our faces, necks, arms, and hands. Michael turned himself mostly yellow and blue. I turned myself lilac, purple, and green. And we listened to the humanoids' and animaloids' heartbeats. We *were* going to get cleaned up when we were through, but we didn't have time. Suddenly Mrs. Galloway and Michael's mom burst in.

They were mad about how we looked. Mrs. Galloway was also mad that I'd said I'd be back at five and it was already a quarter to six. She grabbed me by the arm, dragged me home. "What was that all about?" She wanted to know.

I decided not to complain that she'd wrecked our time. I explained in a nice voice, "We were space doctors giving checkups to non-earthlings."

She said, "What next?" in a nasty voice. Lilac Craypa rubbed off on her dress. She tried wiping it off and started yelling, "See what you did? Get in the bathroom, wash yourself, make yourself look human again—if you can!" She sounded so mean, so mean, I decided it was no use trying to be nice to her.

When I came out of the bathroom, into the kitchen, she was running the cold water—I didn't know what for. She filled up a bowl. I couldn't think why. She put in on the floor. I was so surprised, I could almost not believe it. "Whiskers, come wet your whistle," she called.

Whiskers came running, her heavy sides shaking, and lapped it up with a big thirst.

"Have you noticed how much water she's been wanting these past few days?" asked Mrs. Galloway, and she gave me and Whiskers the friendliest look, as if she'd never done mean things to either of us. And I didn't know *what* to think.

The Big Battle

Sunday, we were out at Grandma Sonia's. One thing we like doing there is rummaging in the attic.

Mom found an old cradle. "Look at this. All my dolls used to sleep in here." We dusted it off. It was still in good shape. It had pink hearts and blue forget-me-nots painted on the headboard, and it was nice and roomy.

We brought it home. Mom thought Whiskers might have her kittens any day now. We both thought the cradle would be a good place. We put in two soft old towels and a piece of an old pink crib blanket of mine. We made it really cozy.

"What's this doing here?" asked Mrs. Galloway on Monday.

I explained. I put Whiskers in. I'd been doing that pretty often, to give her the idea.

She stepped back out of it.

Mrs. Galloway went *Hrrmph* in her throat, and she shrugged her shoulders.

I said, "Don't you think it would make a neat nest for her kittens?"

"The question is, will *she* think so," said Mrs. Galloway in a way I didn't like, as if she knew a whole lot more about what Whiskers would think than I did.

The next afternoon, Michael came over. We were going to play Jungle, and we needed Whiskers to be the panther. We looked and looked, and couldn't find her anywhere. Finally we looked under my bed. There she was, way in the corner.

She never usually hides down there. We

called and called to her. She wouldn't come out. We rolled her toy to her—the one with the silver bell in it. She usually loves chasing it. She wasn't interested.

I got scared that she wasn't feeling well. Then I thought, Hey, maybe . . . !

Michael and I made ourselves very flat and squeezed under my bed to see what she was doing. But it was too dark.

I got my flashlight. We shone it at her. She went *Fawwwgh*, and made a funny motion, turning away, closer to the wall.

I was starting to say, "Hey, Michael, I bet she's—" when all of a sudden—*whhsk!*—Michael slid past me. Mrs. Galloway had grabbed his feet and was yanking him out.

She dragged me out next. "Beds are for sleeping in, not crawling under!"

"But Mrs. Galloway, Whiskers is down there. I think she's starting to have her kittens."

"You nosy kids keep away from her, then!"

"She's *my* cat. I'll do what I want."

"Not while *I'm* here," Mrs. Galloway said quietly, but it sounded fiercer than yelling.

"I'm going home." Michael went.

This was it, I decided: the big battle of our war. "I'm going to see what's happening," I said, and I crawled back under my bed and turned my flashlight on.

Whiskers's eyes blinked shut.

Mrs. Galloway yanked me out. "I told you to leave that cat be!"

"And I told you, she's *my* cat! Under *my* bed, in *my* room! You're so old-fashioned! I know what you think—that children shouldn't watch how kittens get born. Well, I think they should, and I'm going to!"

"Sh. Don't make such a racket."

"Don't shush me! I can make as much noise as I want in here." My room had turned into a battlefield, with two armies, me and her. "You can't stop me!" I tried to duck under again.

"Oh, no?" She swooped me up.

Every part of me was mad at her. My hands made fists, all on their own. My fists lunged. She grabbed my wrists, just in the nick, or she'd have gotten a punch in the stomach.

She stood holding on to me, like I was a prisoner. She said, "Rebecca Suslow, I forbid you to crawl under your bed and bother that cat," in a voice like she was Commander in Chief, Boss Over Everything.

"Let go!"

"If you'll leave that cat alone."

My wrists were hurting. "Okay."

She let go of me. She stood in front of my bed, legs apart, arms out, on guard. I wheeled around and ran into Mom's room.

I dived onto Mom's bed. I started punching numbers on her phone. Mom's number at the hospital is 555-9701. I punched the 5's and the 9. My finger was over the 7.

Mrs. G. came marching in. "Calling your mother, are you?"

I punched the 7 and the 0.

"What if she's in the middle of sewing up a cut on somebody's chin? Or setting a broken elbow? And she has to say to the person, 'Oh, excuse me, I have to go talk on the telephone'?"

I said, "Look, Mom gave me her number

to use in an emergency. And this is an emergency."

"Is that right? Are some burglars climbing in the window? Is the kitchen on fire? Is the apartment-house roof caving in?" She put her hands on her hips. "What emergency, may I ask?"

"Whiskers's kittens are getting born! And you won't let me see. Maybe it's hurting Whiskers. Mom's delivered babies, she could help, she'd know what to do!"

The Lucky Scarf

Mrs. Galloway sat down, not on Mom's bed—at least she had the sense to know she shouldn't sit there—but on the chair next to it.

She tried to take my hands. I pulled them away. "Now you listen to me." Good thing she didn't call me Becca. Or I'd have clapped my hands over my ears and kept my ears shut till she quit talking. "Whiskers knows what to do. Having kittens doesn't hurt cats. They don't need doctors. They can take care of the whole thing by themselves. All they need is a comfortable place and to be left alone."

"How do *you* know such a lot about it? It's not that comfortable under my bed."

"Not for you and Michael. But for a cat it's nice and private, and away from the light."

"But the floor's too hard."

"I put some soft things there for her."

"The stuff from the cradle? Who said you could?"

"No, just some clean rags and an old scarf of mine. . . . "

"You did? When? How did you know that's where she'd have her kittens?"

"She's been going down there, spending time there for a while. I thought you knew."

"You put a scarf of *yours* there for her? Really?"

"Mm-hm. My old good-luck scarf."

"How is it a good-luck scarf?"

"A cat of mine once took a liking to it."

"*You* had a cat?"

"Quite a few. Before we moved to an apartment."

"How come you never said so?"

"You never asked," said Mrs. Galloway.

I thought, Wait a minute, let me get this straight! And I asked, "Did you make the cat who took a liking to your scarf eat lots of Tunafeast?"

"I didn't 'make' her. It was her favorite brand."

"Did you push her down off your furniture? Dump her out of your bureau drawers?"

"A couple of times, you bet. Till she caught on where she was allowed and where not."

"What was her name?"

"Fitzcatrick."

"Isn't that a name for a tom?"

"We thought so, but she surprised us."

"You mean, by having kittens?"

"Right. And guess where she had them."

"On your lucky scarf?"

"Exactly. The finest litter of kittens you ever saw."

"I've never seen any litter of kittens! Come on, Mrs. Galloway, can't I go see how Whiskers is doing?"

"How about putting the phone back?" she said.

I didn't realize it was still on my lap. I put it on Mom's night table.

"Okay, if you'll be very quiet."

We went into my room. Mrs. G. lifted up the dust ruffle in a few places so just a little bit of light would come under the bed. And we got down on all fours and we peeked.

"I think one's already born! Oh, please, let me go closer!"

"Uh-uh." She held on to me.

"I want to see it, so badly!"

"You will. When she's through."

"When will that be?"

"I don't know. It could take a couple of hours. Then she'll want you to see them. She'll bring them out herself and show them to you. When she's good and ready." Mrs. G. pulled me up to my feet, put her hands on my shoulders. They didn't feel too bad there. "Just be a little patient, Reb."

Reb. Hm. That was a new one. Nobody'd ever called me by that name before.

Between then and six-fifteen, just to pass
the time, I helped her peel potatoes and I scraped
and cut up carrots for a stew. While she
browned the meat, she told about Fitzcatrick's
kittens. There were four. She and Mr. Galloway still lived in a house then, and their cats
could go outside. They kept two kittens for
themselves. The other two they gave to their
"kids"—the ones she'd "walloped, good," when
they were little. But now they were grown up
and on their own.

When Mom came home I raced to tell her,
"Mom, Mom, guess what!"

"Phew, I'm really tired," Mom said. "Let
me get out of these clothes first and take a
shower, okay?"

While Mom took her shower, Mrs. G. and
I took another look under the bed. "Three—
wow, great!"

"Sh." Mrs. G. put her hand over my mouth.
"Don't scare them."

"I can't wait to see them," I said into her
hand, "can you?"

Then Mom took a look. And she agreed

with Mrs. Galloway that we should leave Whiskers and her kittens alone, in privacy.

Mom and I had *our* private time.

Mrs. Galloway got ready to leave.

I asked her, "Don't you want to hang around a little while?"

She said, "Yes, I'd like to, for just a bit." She went into the kitchen.

Mom said, "Mm, I smell stew."

"Right. I helped make it. Mom, we should invite Mrs. G. to stay and have dinner with us tonight."

Mom said, "I can't believe my ears. Did you really say that?"

"Yes. I think she wants to be here when Whiskers brings the kittens out."

Mom said, "Fine."

Mrs. Galloway looked really happy when I invited her. But she couldn't stay. Her husband is the manager at a bowling alley. Usually he works nights. But he had that evening off and they were going out to a restaurant.

"Oh." And for the first time since she became my sitter, I was kind of sorry when she had to go.

All through the stew I kept looking at the kitchen door, hoping to see Whiskers. We were almost through with our dessert when she finally appeared. And she showed us the kittens, one by one by one.

They looked like pink balls with little bits of fur on. The first one was going to be mostly white, you could tell, and had wide, wide-apart eyes, which of course were not open yet.

The second was tiger-striped with tiny pointy ears sticking up.

The third, I was sure, was going to be all black, with a white tip on the tail. The way Whiskers carried it in, if it could have opened its eyes right then, it would have looked straight up at me.

While Whiskers was showing it to Mom, I went under my bed for just a second. I took the scarf out from there—it was okay, the kittens weren't on it.

It's old-looking, with some rips in it. But it's very soft and cuddly, with red, blue, green, and yellow polka dots.

I dangled it in front of Whiskers. Then I put it on the cradle. I wanted to give her the idea of moving the kittens there.

But she liked it better under my bed. That stayed their headquarters. And in the middle of the night she went and took the lucky scarf out of the cradle and brought it back down there.

That night, before I went to bed, Mom asked me, "How's your war with Mrs. Galloway?" She was teasing. She knew it was just about over.

And just before I fell asleep, I got this idea. . . .

I didn't burst right out with it. First I had some talks with Mrs. Galloway, about cats' lives in little apartments. She thinks cats should have plenty of room to roam around in. Sure, I agree. But suppose they don't have a home. Wouldn't a little apartment be a whole lot better for cats like that than nowhere at all?

I also asked about the bowling alley where Mr. Galloway worked. Were there any mice or rats there that a cat could keep away? Also, I watched how she acted around the kittens. . . .

One day when they were two and a half weeks old and already had their eyes open wide and were getting pretty playful, Michael and I were teaching them to reach for balloons at the ends of strings. Michael was sad when he had to go home. He really wanted one.

Mrs. G. said, "Maybe, if you ask your mother at just the right moment, she'll change her mind."

After Michael left, and Mrs. G. and I were sitting together pretty cozily in the kitchen, I asked her, "By the way, how would *you* like to have a kitten?"

"Who, me?" I don't know. . . . " She stretched her legs way forward, sat way back in her chair, let her head droop over backward, and gave a kind of sigh, but not a sad one.

"You could pick out whichever one you like

best." (I was holding the black one with the white-tipped tail in my lap.) "You could call it your favorite name."

"I'll have to think about it," she said.

Cat Family Reunion

We kept all three kittens till they were six weeks old.

Today it's three months since the day they were born. Mom ordered a cake at Dominic's Bakery. They make cakes for all sorts of occasions.

Michael's mother *did* change her mind. She let Michael take a kitten: the mostly white one with wide-apart eyes. She wet the floor, she made a mess, as soon as Michael brought her into their apartment. "What a catastrophe!" said his mom. Catastrophe means very bad disaster. Michael liked the sound of it, so they named their kitten that. Strophe, for short. The way you say that is, you make it rhyme with Sophie.

Mrs. Galloway picked the tiger-striped one with pointy ears. She named it Reb. I'm its godmother.

I have the black one with the white-tipped tail, and white paws, too, and her hind legs look as though she's wearing knee socks, just like her mom. When she was eight days old, and opened her eyes for the very first time, I happened to be sitting on my floor, watching her. So the very first thing she saw in her whole life was me. I named her Deborah.

Any minute now, Michael's coming over, with Strophe. Reb's already here, and so is Deborah, of course.

The cake is chocolate with strawberry icing. It says "Happy Birthday, Kittens." But it's really for us humans to have, while their family has its reunion.